Hiding Dinosaurs

Dan Moynihan

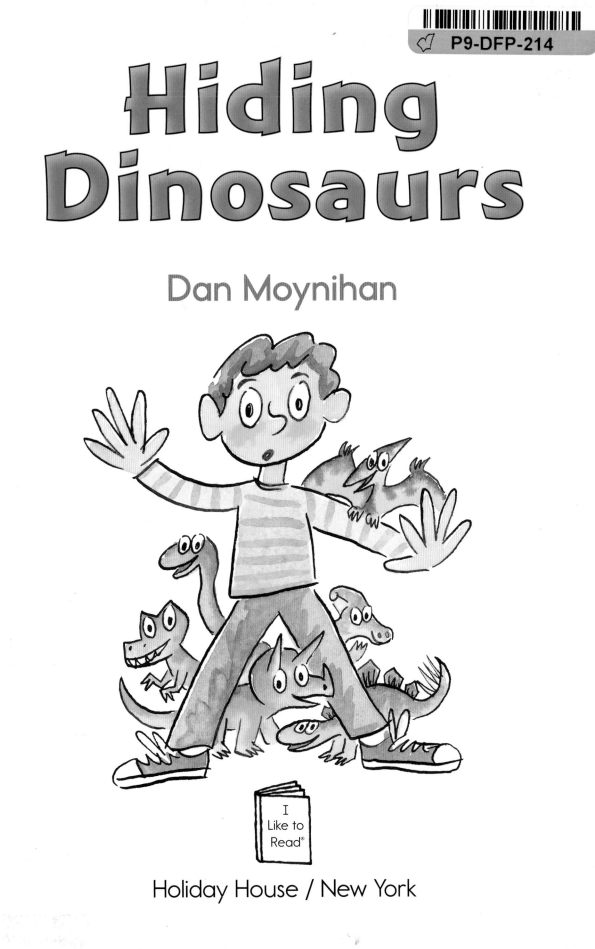

I Like to Read®

Holiday House / New York

*For my parents, who allowed me
to keep as many dinosaurs
in the house as I wanted*

I LIKE TO READ is a registered trademark of Holiday House, Inc.

Copyright © 2015 by Dan Moynihan
All Rights Reserved
HOLIDAY HOUSE is registered in the U.S. Patent and Trademark Office.
Printed and Bound in April 2015 at Tien Wah Press, Johor Bahru, Johor, Malaysia.
The artwork was created with pen and ink and watercolors.
www.holidayhouse.com
First Edition
1 3 5 7 9 10 8 6 4 2

Library of Congress Cataloging-in-Publication Data
Moynihan, Dan, 1973-
Hiding dinosaurs / by Dan Moynihan. — First edition.
pages cm. — (I like to read)
Summary: After watching six dinosaurs hatch, a boy tries to keep them hidden as they grow up.
ISBN 978-0-8234-3196-0 (hardcover)
[1. Dinosaurs—Fiction. 2. Growth—Fiction.] I. Title.
PZ7.M8674Hid 2015
[E]—dc23
2013050737

ISBN 978-0-8234-3421-3 (paperback)

It was time for breakfast.
But the eggs were too old.

So we had cereal.

At lunchtime
I saw something odd.

The eggs were moving.

They hatched.

I gave them some lunch.
They liked that.

I had to hide them from Mom.

That was close.
I took the dinosaurs
to my room.

The dinosaurs liked my room.

I wanted to keep them.

But Mom was coming.

I had to think fast.

Then I hid them under my bed.

That was good for a while.
But the dinosaurs grew.

And they grew.
Soon they were too big
to hide under my bed.

I tried to keep the dinosaurs
in my room.

One day I couldn't hide my dinosaurs anymore. Mom and Dad were surprised.

And I was surprised . . .

because Mom and Dad
love dinosaurs too.

And so do my friends!